The Road to Hidden Harbor

The Road to Hidden Harbor

ANNE STUART

THORNDIKE
CHIVERS

This Large Print edition is published by Thorndike Press®, Waterville, Maine USA and by BBC Audiobooks, Ltd, Bath, England.

Published in 2003 in the U.S. by arrangement with Harlequin Books, S.A.

Published in 2003 in the U.K. by arrangement with Harlequin Enterprises II, B.V.

U.S. Hardcover 0-7862-6088-2 (Romance)
U.K. Hardcover 0-7540-7765-9 (Chivers Large Print)
U.K. Softcover 0-7540-7766-7 (Camden Large Print)

The text of this Large Print edition is unabridged.
Other aspects of the book may vary from the original edition.

Set in 16 pt. Plantin by Ramona Watson.

Printed in the United States on permanent paper.

British Library Cataloguing-in-Publication Data available

Library of Congress Cataloging-in-Publication Data

Stuart, Anne (Anne Kristine)
    The road to Hidden Harbor / Anne Stuart.
    p. cm.
    ISBN 0-7862-6088-2 (lg. print : hc : alk. paper)
    1. College teachers — Fiction. 2. English teachers — Fiction. 3. Missing persons — Fiction. 4. Women teachers — Fiction. 5. Biographers — Fiction. 6. Maine — Fiction. 7. Poets — Fiction. 8. Large type books.
I. Title.
PS3569.T785R63 2003
813′.54—dc22
                            2003065092

The Road to
Hidden Harbor

CHAPTER ONE

Molly Ferrell pulled her car to a stop on the bluff overlooking the ocean, switching off the engine and putting the stick shift in first gear. She'd been sitting in her cramped little Honda for the better part of two days, and she was finally within sight of her destination. Hidden Harbor, Maine, was a small town halfway up the seacoast, nestled between two spits of land, and even in the bustling new millennium it still remained relatively secluded.

Of course, it wasn't high summer. Autumn had come, turning the leaves to shades of gold and brass and copper, the summer vacationers had departed, and most of the inns and bed-and-breakfasts had closed for the season. She'd been lucky to find a place to stay. There was always the larger town of Sanford some thirty miles away, but that wouldn't have been half as effective. She needed to live in Hidden Harbor itself. To find the answers she needed.

She'd had to make her reservation the old-fashioned way, by telephone, since the Internet had proven surprisingly unhelpful. Just when she was ready to give in and call the Sanford Holiday Inn, her luck had changed. The Harbor Inn was closed for repair and renovations, but the owner, Marjorie Twitchell, could offer her a room and not much else if she was willing to rough it.

Molly would have pitched a tent on the town green if she had to. She'd managed to finagle three months leave to finish her research. By January she'd be back teaching at the huge educational factory that was Southern Michigan University, and she was going to have to work fast if she was at least going to have a decent outline for her book under her belt. Though deep in her heart of hearts she was hoping for a rough draft.

It was time to get on with her life. Time to put away childish things. Her near obsession for a long-dead writer was just that — a remnant from her dreamy-eyed adolescence. If she ever wanted to make tenure then she had to let go of the ghost of Michael O'Flannery. And she'd come to Hidden Harbor to do just that.

Why couldn't she have had a crush on

someone normal, like an actor or a rock star instead of a relatively obscure poet? Michael O'Flannery had lived and died shrouded in mystery, and only the barest details had surfaced, most of them suspect. In the twenty years since he'd killed himself he'd been almost forgotten. One brilliant novel and a collection of gorgeous, morbid poetry could only carry a reputation so far. His mysterious death added to the allure, as had his youth, but even that had faded in the past few years, making O'Flannery nothing more than a literary footnote. And leaving a strange, impractical obsession that had started when she was an impressionable fifteen-year-old and still haunted her more than a decade later. She loved his words and his images, the quirky way his mind had worked. She loved everything about him, including his tragic fate.

If she could find the truth then maybe she could let go of him. Tear his short, brilliant life into little pieces to be examined and prodded and then packed away.

She was ready to move on, ready to turn past lost poets, past broken engagements, past dreamy vulnerability into hardheaded practicality.

It was time she grew up. Once she made

tenure she wouldn't want to leave the university. Wouldn't dare to leave that kind of security. If she was going to have choices in her life she needed to do something about it now, before it was too late.

The town of Hidden Harbor looked peaceful from her vantage point. There were no fancy yachts moored in the harbor — only sturdy fishing boats. Lobster boats most likely. She knew from her research that lobstering was the major industry in the small town. Those who didn't work in the trade were pretty much destitute. Like Michael O'Flannery's drunken father.

None of his family had survived him — he'd had no siblings, no aunts or uncles, and his parents had died in a car accident before he'd killed himself. But there'd be neighbors. People who'd been there when he'd grown up, who'd have stories, memories. Who might know something that would lead to the truth about Michael O'Flannery. What demons had driven him to write such dark, haunted prose? And what had driven him to take a gun and walk into the woods, never to be seen again?

If she were really lucky she might even find a photograph of him. He'd been notoriously camera shy during his short time in the spotlight, and the only pictures that remained were shots of the back of his head. She'd spent years of her life fantasizing about someone and she didn't even know what he looked like.

In a way, that had been part of his appeal. He could be anything she wanted — tall, short, lean, muscle-bound, close-cropped dark hair or long blond curls. It was one more way she was able to convince herself she was in love with his words, not the man himself. How could you love someone you'd never even seen?

She took a deep breath, the tang of the salt sea air in her lungs. It had been years since she'd even seen the ocean. She'd forgotten how oddly soothing it was, to sit and watch the waves batter against the rocks. Lake Michigan, vast and beautiful as it was, just didn't cut it.

She'd grown up in a small, coastal town on Rhode Island, right on the water, and she would have thought she'd had enough of the ocean's vast changeability. She'd forgotten how it got in your veins and stayed there. She looked down at the quiet fishing village. She'd never been there in her life, and yet it felt like home. The ocean called to her, almost as strongly as Michael O'Flannery's legend, and she realized for

11

the first time she wanted to come back. To live by the sea again. It wasn't going to be any time soon. She couldn't afford ocean-front property any more than she could abandon teaching. But this would be a taste of it, enough to tide her over for a few years.

She climbed back in her car, shoving her hair away from her face. "I'm going to find you, Michael O'Flannery," she murmured. "I'm going to find your ghost and every-thing I can about you. Just watch me."

There was no answer on the sharp ocean breeze. But then, she hadn't expected one. She turned the key, put the car in gear and started down the winding road to Hidden Harbor.

It was easy enough to find the Harbor Inn. There wasn't much to the town — people probably drove over to nearby San-ford for shopping or movies. Half the houses were shuttered and closed up against the coming winter, and even though the weather was still relatively warm there was a cold, dark feeling to the place.

She was being melodramatic, a weakness of hers, Molly thought. It was nothing more than a seaside community reacting to the economic realities of the changing seasons. A bit smaller than usual, a bit more behind the times. The place probably hadn't changed much in the last thirty years, unlike the rest of the seacoast. Maybe not in the last fifty years.

Which would suit her just fine. The town would have looked the same when Michael O'Flannery was growing up. She would finally begin to know what his life had actually been like.

It was late afternoon, and the shadows on the empty streets were long and somber. The Harbor Inn was at one end of the town, overlooking the harbor and the vast Atlantic beyond it. It was a large, rambling building, in dire need of paint and a new roof. She could hear the muffled sounds of hammers and power tools as she pulled up in the empty parking lot, and she winced. Marjorie Twitchell had warned her there'd be noise and dust, but Molly hadn't really had any choice in the matter. Besides, the inn was more than a hundred years old. O'Flannery himself must have been inside that building during his short lifetime. She'd actually be under the same roof where he may have once been. Breathe the same air, walk the same floors. The thought was disturbingly exciting.

So she was a little obsessed. What was

13

the problem with that? It was good to get involved in your work, wasn't it? O'Flannery was simply a fascinating character study. Anyone would be caught up in the legend and drama. Her former fiancé had once told her in a jealous fit that she was in love with O'Flannery. Well, maybe she was, just a little bit. He was long dead — what harm would a little fantasy do her? Except that Robert always insisted that as long as she loved O'Flannery she'd never love him.

Well, she had more reason than ever to love her lost poet. Robert was a jerk, and she was well rid of him. It was her pride that was hurt, not her heart. Which for some reason made it even worse.

She hauled her suitcase and laptop out of the car and headed for the front door. It was thick, solid wood, and she doubted her knocking would carry very far over the sounds of carpentry. There was no bell, but after a moment she tried the polished brass doorknob. It wasn't locked.

She stepped into the hall, dumping her luggage on the faded Oriental carpet, and caught her breath. It was like stepping into another century. Dust motes danced in the air, and she could smell the years mixing with the tang of the ocean and the sweet scent of fresh lumber. If anyone could bottle that fragrance they'd make a fortune, Molly thought. When she made her way back to Michigan she'd only have the memory of that evocative smell.

"Hello?" she called into the rambling old house. Her voice probably didn't penetrate much farther than her knocking had. She closed the door behind her, shutting the world outside, and headed in the direction of the noise.

She found the source of the voices easily enough in the torn-apart kitchen. She pushed open a door and the sudden silence was shocking.

"You must be Dr. Ferrell!" A plump, middle-aged woman stepped forward, a nervous smile on her face. "Welcome to Hidden Harbor! I'm sorry I didn't hear you knock — Jake and Davy have been making a terrible racket. I'm Marjorie Twitchell, of course, and these two are my carpenters, Jake and Davy. Jake, this is Molly Ferrell. Remember, I told you she'd be staying here for the next few weeks?"

"You told me," the man said. "You just neglected to tell me why until five minutes ago."

He turned and looked at her, and the hostility in his dark blue eyes was startling.

15

She'd never seen the man in her life, but he'd already decided he didn't like her.

"Now, Jake . . ." Mrs. Twitchell began in a plaintive voice.

But Jake wasn't listening to her — he was concentrating the full force of his attention on Molly. He was good-looking, maybe ten years older than she was, with long dark hair and cold eyes and good bones. Not that she was interested — she'd sworn off everyone but Michael O'Flannery for the next three months. And clearly this man was even less impressed with her.

"She's here to dig up old bones and to poke her nose where it doesn't belong." He had a deep, implacable voice, one that sent an odd little shiver down her spine.

"I'm not here to do any such thing," she protested. "Michael O'Flannery was a wonderful writer, and I don't want his work lost and forgotten."

Jake simply looked at her for a long moment. It made her nervous. "Maybe he's better off forgotten. Let him rest in peace."

"I can't," she said simply.

"What's she talking about, Jake?" She hadn't seen the other man standing in the shadows, which was astonishing, since he was huge, even taller than Jake, massive and hulking. He was looking at her out of

16

wide, childlike eyes, and he moved into the light with a shambling gait, a mix of curiosity and hostility etched on his face.

"Nothing, Davy," Jake said in a calm voice. "She's just another tourist."

"The tourists are gone. What's she got to do with Michael? Is she going to bring him back?"

"Michael's not coming back, Davy. He's been dead and gone for twenty years, remember?"

"I remember," Davy said. He took another step toward her. "She's pretty."

"Davy!" Jake's deep voice held a warning, but Davy wasn't listening. He moved across the kitchen, coming straight toward her. "She's pretty, Jake," he said in his singsong voice, "I don't think we need to worry."

It was enough to make Jake move. He crossed the room and took Davy's arm, pulling him away from her with surprisingly gentle hands.

"There's nothing to worry about anyway, Davy," he said patiently. "I'll take you home now."

"But we have more work to do."

"We can wait until after she's gone."

"I'm not going to be in anyone's way," Molly said. Jake's blue eyes slid over her, and

17

she controlled her nervous start. "I'll be out talking to people, doing research . . ."

"You're wasting your time here," he said. "Marjorie should have told you that. You should never have come here in the first place."

"I beg your pardon?" she said, trying to summon her frostiest voice.

He was cold enough to begin with. "You heard me," he said. "No one's going to tell you a damned thing. Come on, Davy."

And the door slammed shut behind him.

"Oh, my," Mrs. Twitchell said. "He has such a temper. I should have warned you Jake might be a bit difficult. Just pay him no mind, dear. He'll get over it."

"What's his problem?"

"The same problem you'll encounter wherever you go," she said in her cheerful little voice. "Michael O'Flannery."

It could have been worse, Jake thought, once he dropped Davy off at his parents' house. There'd been other academics over the years, showing up in Hidden Harbor, asking questions, prying through things. Molly Ferrell was younger than most, and she didn't have that hard-edged, professional quality to her. As a matter of fact, she didn't look like a professor at all, though

Marjorie Twitchell had assured him she was.

She was young — maybe late twenties. No more than ten years younger than he was, but a generation apart. She was pretty, too, in a soft, unspectacular way. Unfortunately he'd always been a sucker for warm brown eyes and long brown hair. And he couldn't help noticing her mouth.

He shook his head. He knew better than to let a pair of beautiful eyes distract him. So she was pretty. He was a healthy male who'd been surrounded by the same women for too long. It was only natural that he'd be . . . distracted by her.

But that was only a temporary reaction. She was trouble, despite her quiet voice and almost shy demeanor. She was here to poke her nose into places it didn't belong, and he needed to get rid of her, just as he'd gotten rid of the others over the years.

He didn't want to do it, but he would. Some things were just too precious to risk. The truth being one of them.

CHAPTER TWO

The breeze had picked up, scudding the dry leaves down the empty sidewalk. Molly pulled her heavy wool sweater up around her ears, wishing she'd brought a hat and gloves. The cold air had a lot more bite when it swept in across the Atlantic, and Indian summer seemed to have deserted Hidden Harbor.

So had most of its inhabitants.

She had been planning a short walk from the old inn through the center of the small town and back, just enough to stretch her legs and get the stiffness out of her body. Just enough to give her time to think about Mrs. Twitchell's startling revelation.

At first she thought the old lady was imagining things. Why should anyone care about a long-dead misfit? As far as Molly knew, she was the only one who even remembered Michael O'Flannery had existed, and she'd gotten used to the notion that he was her private possession. But the unfriendly Jake had certainly taken an immediate dislike to her, and every inhabitant of Hidden Harbor seemed to have disappeared at her approach. Businesses were closed, shades were pulled.

She trudged on, keeping her head down against the sharp breeze. It had to be her imagination — after all, it was just after five. Most businesses would be closed.

And most people would be out on the streets, on their way home. Except that this was a fishing community, she reminded herself. Lobster fisherman wouldn't go by the clock.

The town of Hidden Harbor was less than three blocks long. At the end was a town green, and behind it a tall white church, its spire reaching heavenward at a slightly askew angle. She crossed the empty green to pause at the iron gate outside the churchyard. It was Presbyterian, and O'Flannery had been raised a Catholic. He wouldn't have come here during his short life. But for some reason she opened the latch and walked in.

The graveyard was surprisingly well tended. The dead leaves had been raked, the weeds trimmed, no broken headstones or tacky plastic flowers. She passed Twitchells and Thomases, Morrisons and Matthews, Bairds and Belhams, some

21

dating back to the seventeen hundreds. She was wandering aimlessly, she told herself, but her feet had a mind of their own. And as if she were drawn there, she found herself exactly where she knew she'd end up, in front of a stark, black marble headstone.

Michael J. O'Flannery, 1963–1983. Nothing else. The dates were right, but what in heaven's name was he doing being buried in a Presbyterian cemetery? For that matter, what was he doing being buried at all? No one had ever found his body, or indeed, any trace of him. There was nothing lying in the ground beneath the stark headstone, so why had someone gone to the expense and bother? He'd had no family left to care.

A few dead leaves had drifted in front of the stone, and on impulse she knelt and began to brush them away. He wasn't there, but she felt the strange need to touch him, touch the stone that was somehow connected to him . . .

"What the hell are you doing?"

She pulled her hand away fast, straightening up so quickly she almost slammed into him. It was her nemesis from the hotel, Jake the carpenter, looking down at her with all the warmth of a hungry python.

"Er . . ." she said with great brilliance, but he wasn't really looking for an answer.

"Why don't you leave him alone?" he demanded. "He was hounded enough in his lifetime, and he doesn't need academic groupies moping at his grave."

That stung. "How did you know who I was?"

"You look like a groupie."

"I mean, how did you know I was an academic?" she said hastily.

"Marjorie told me. You're not the first one, you know. Others have come here before you, looking for scandal, looking for lost masterpieces from the great man." His sarcastic tone was infuriating. "You're squat out of luck. There's nothing left. He's dead, go away."

"Why are you trying to get rid of me, Mr. . . . ?"

"Just call me Jake. You're going to be seeing a lot of me."

She blinked. "What do you mean by that?"

"I'm going to be dogging your footsteps, lady. We don't like people messing with our local hero, and I intend to make sure you don't cause any trouble."

She wondered for a brief moment if the man was a raving lunatic. He seemed sane enough, in a good-looking, bad-tempered sort of way. She decided to try reason. "I have no intention of causing any trouble. I'm planning on writing a book about O'Flannery, but it's about his work, not about his life."

"Then why are you here? His books are still in print — go buy them."

"I have them. Every edition. But the facts of his life inform his works, and I just want to —"

"You just want to snoop around. Weep at his grave, nose into his past, talk to his lovers."

"Lovers?" she perked up at that. "I never thought of that." Maybe it was because she wasn't sure she liked the idea of Michael O'Flannery actually having sexual relationships. "Male or female?"

"What?"

"There were rumors that he was gay, and that's why he killed himself."

The man rolled his eyes in total disgust. "He wasn't gay. And even twenty years ago people didn't tend to kill themselves over their sexual orientation. You've got an overactive imagination, Dr. Ferrell."

"So I've been told. And see, you've already proven yourself wrong. You said I wouldn't learn anything about O'Flannery from anyone, and yet you've already told me he wasn't gay. You must have known him." The more she thought about it the more she warmed to the idea. "You're probably around the same age he would have been. Did you grow up with him? Were you friends?"

He grimaced. "Get out of here. If you know what's good for you, you'll leave town. Who he was doesn't matter. His work is the only thing that counted, and you already have that."

"Thank you for your concern, but I have no intention of leaving anytime soon," she said calmly. "At least not until I find out why a few simple questions seem to throw people into a fit. You in particular."

"Don't say I didn't warn you."

"Oh, you've warned me," she said cheerfully. "Over and over again. I just wonder why."

"Maybe I don't want any more unsolved deaths in Hidden Harbor." And he turned and walked away.

She stood there, frozen, watching him leave. If she weren't so shocked she would have raced after him, demanding an explanation. Unsolved deaths? Was he suggesting that O'Flannery was murdered? Or was he talking about someone else?

And even more important, was he threatening her?

She shook her head. He was right, she had much too vivid an imagination. No one would want to hurt her for asking a few impertinent questions. No one would be forced to answer them — they could simply ignore her. They already seemed to be doing just that.

She looked down at the grave. There were no flowers and no epitaph, just the dates bringing a stark reminder of how short a life he'd had. And she wanted, needed to know why.

She started back through the deserted town, hands jammed in her pockets, deep in thought. Lights spilled out on the sidewalk from one business that obviously hadn't heard The Pariah had come to town, and she stopped, staring into the cozy interior of Binnie's Diner.

Maybe it was all her imagination. Maybe Jake was crazy. And maybe she really needed a cup of coffee and a bowl of soup.

She pushed open the door, and voices spilled out with the warmth and the light. By the time she closed the door behind her all noise had stopped, except for the hiss and splatter of the grill.

There must have been eight or nine

people in the small restaurant, most of them at the long counter, and they were all staring at her. The expression on their faces was the same — distrust and unwelcome, and for a bizarre moment, she thought they were all part of the same, identical inbred family.

When they turned away from her, she realized that the only similarity they had was their wariness toward her. A skinny woman stood behind the counter, glaring at her, her too-bright lipstick garish in the fluorescent light. "We're closed," she said.

Molly had excellent eyesight, and she could read the name Binnie embroidered across the woman's flat breast. She glanced around at the other patrons, who were busily applying themselves to their food. Her gaze skittered over to the waitress, who looked up at Molly and smiled as she set a plate of food on one of the tables.

"We aren't closing yet, Binnie," she said in a cheery voice. "It's cold out there — we're not going to refuse a stranger a cup of coffee, are we?"

The last thing Molly wanted to do was to sit down in front of all those staring eyes and try to choke something down, but pride kept her rooted to the floor. If she let them drive her away this early, then she wouldn't accomplish a thing. And this was one thing she needed to finish.

"Suit yourself," Binnie said in a sour voice, turning back to the grill.

"There's a nice booth over in the corner," the waitress said. Her name was emblazoned across her chest, as well, though her relative curviness made it a little harder to read. It was either Laura Ann or Laura Jane, but Molly decided she couldn't spend too much time staring at a strange woman's breast — she'd already made enough enemies in this town just by being here.

"Thanks," she said. She made her way through the crowded restaurant to the empty table and slunk into the seat. The people of Hidden Harbor were starting to talk again, albeit in low, hushed voices as they shot occasional glances her way. By the time Molly opened up the menu, Laura was back, with two cups of coffee and a friendly smile.

She set both cups down on the table and slid into the seat opposite her. "Welcome to Hidden Harbor, Dr. Ferrell. Don't mind the others — they're not really that unfriendly once you get to know them."

A muffled "humph" accompanied Laura Jane's cheerful statement. She lowered her voice. "It's just that everyone around here feels a little protective about Michael's memory. They're worried about what you might say."

Molly took a tentative sip of her coffee. She usually drank it black, but this stuff had the consistency of tar, and she reached for the creamer. "Aren't you going to get into trouble talking to me?"

Laura Jane grinned. "I've lived in this town all my life — they're used to me by now. All the disapproval in the world isn't going to shut me up."

"All your life? Did you know Michael O'Flannery?"

Laura Jane laughed. "Straight to the point, aren't you? Let me give you a little advice. People around here like plain speaking, but you'd still better take it slow if you want to get somewhere. We don't give up our secrets easily."

Molly wrapped her hands around the thick mug, taking her time. "There are secrets?" she asked.

"There are always secrets," Laura Jane said. "And, yes. I knew Michael. I was desperately in love with him. So was the entire female population of Hidden Harbor, young and old. Who wouldn't be? He was beautiful and tortured and wildly romantic.

You're probably a little bit in love with him yourself."

Molly jerked, startled. That was the second time in less than an hour that someone had accused her of being in love with Michael O'Flannery. She wasn't, of course. At most she had a kind of silly crush on him, but she hadn't thought it was that pitifully obvious. "It's pretty much a waste of time to be in love with a dead man, wouldn't you say?" she murmured, taking a sip of her coffee and managing not to shudder.

"You wouldn't be the first," she said. "By the way, I'm Laura Jane Twitchell. Your landlady's my mother-in-law. You'll find that most people around here are related."

"Then that would explain Michael O'Flannery's headstone. I thought all his family had died."

"They did. Before he killed himself. The town thought they'd erect that monument. The people around here felt kind of bad about the way they treated him."

"What do you mean?"

Before she could answer, the door to the café opened, and Jake stepped inside. The quiet hum of conversation stopped once again, as everyone turned to look at him.

And then looked at her. And then back at him, as if it were some macabre tennis match.

The moment his eyes set on Laura Jane she scrambled from the bench. "Guess my break's over," she said cheerfully. "Hi, there, Marley. What can I get you?"

"Peace and quiet," he muttered.

Laura Jane wasn't the slightest intimidated by Jake's attitude. "We're kind of crowded tonight. Why don't you sit with Dr. Ferrell?"

The audible gasp from the assembled patrons almost made Molly giggle. What the hell did they think Jake was, the Keeper of the Eternal Flame? He seemed to have appointed himself just that.

Jake simply sat at the counter, turning his back to Molly's table.

"Laura Jane, don't you think you oughta get your fat butt in gear?" Binnie demanded harshly. "We're full up and you're busy flapping your gums."

"Now, Binnie, you know you always wanted a butt like mine," Laura Jane shot back, unperturbed.

"Half of it would do," Binnie snapped.

There was uneasy laughter in the crowded restaurant. Apparently this was an old argument, one that never failed to amuse Binnie's patrons, and for the moment Molly's presence was forgotten.

She leaned back in the booth, letting her eyes wander around the room. Both Laura Jane and Binnie looked as if they were late thirties or early forties. Laura Jane said she and everyone else had been in love with Michael O'Flannery. Presumably that meant Binnie, as well. Is that what Jake had meant when he talked about lovers?

At least Laura Jane's good humor wasn't dampened by the town's disapproval. Once the others realized she meant no harm they'd come around, too. She just needed to be patient.

What was she hoping for, now that she was here? Some kind of ghostly apparition? She was much too practical for that — there was no such thing as ghosts. But she believed in spirits, memories haunting a place. O'Flannery had lived and died in this tiny little town, and it didn't take a boatload of imagination to feel his presence lingering beyond death.

She sure as hell didn't want his transparent shape to appear at her bedside tonight, wrapped in chains and moaning.

Well, maybe she wouldn't mind if his more substantial shape appeared at her bedside. She shook her head. She had to be crazy, daydreaming about ghosts.

It wasn't as if she spent her time fantasizing about O'Flannery. Granted, there'd been a few erotic dreams over the years, but a girl couldn't be held responsible for her subconscious mind. Besides, when O'Flannery killed himself, he was twenty years old, making him too young for her. Even if he were a substantial ghost, what did she have in common with a twenty-year-old?

She glanced at Jake's back. His dark hair was too long, with a streak of premature gray. His shoulders were strong beneath the worn flannel shirt, and she could see his hands wrapped around the mug of coffee. Like the rest of him, his hands were long, lean and beautiful.

She almost knocked over her coffee in her haste to escape from her own thoughts. Who the hell did she want to sleep with — Michael O'Flannery's ghost or Jake's unfriendly presence? Hell, she didn't want to sleep with anyone at all. Sex caused nothing but trouble, and it wasn't worth the fleeting pleasure and comfort. She needed to remember that.

Laura Jane hadn't brought her a bill, so she had no choice but to approach the counter. And the only free space was beside Jake's silent figure.

He didn't move, didn't turn to look at her. She accidentally brushed up against him, and the sensation was oddly unnerving, even through her thick wool sweater. Binnie was studiously ignoring her, but Laura Jane bustled over.

"What do I owe you for the coffee?" Molly's voice came out a bit strained and she cleared her throat. It was no wonder she was tense, faced with an unfriendly crowd of townspeople. The moody man beside her had nothing to do with it.

"On the house," Laura Jane said cheerfully. "Welcome to Hidden Harbor."

"Er . . . thanks," Molly said, trying to ignore the hostility radiating from the man beside her. Trying to ignore the heat.

"Come again!" Laura Jane called as Molly opened the door to the cool dark night.

"Harrumph!" said Binnie.

Jake could feel some of the tension slip away as the door closed behind her. The rest of Binnie's patrons went back to their conversations, but Laura Jane still stood in front of him, with that look on her face that he knew too well.

"Stop it," he said.

"Stop what?"

"Stop looking at me like that. I'm trying to get rid of her," he growled.

"You're doing a piss-poor job of it. Nothing like a little mysterious hatred to keep a woman's interest up. Unless that's what you really want?"

Laura Jane had been a romantic all her life, and marriage and kids hadn't changed her. "I want her out of here, before she finds out anything she shouldn't be finding out."

"Maybe." She didn't sound convinced. "You're going about it the wrong way then. You're acting like you've got something to hide. We all are. The best way to distract her is to help her. You're smart enough to know that."

"Help her find the truth about Michael O'Flannery?"

"Help her find out what she wants to know. You've got a good imagination, Jake Marley. I'm sure you'll think of something. Some cracking good yarn that she'll swallow whole and make her forget all about Michael's mysterious disappearance. You're a good storyteller."

He grimaced. "Maybe I don't feel like cozying up to her."

"And maybe you do, which is part of the problem. You forget, I've known you all your life. You like her."

"She's a pain in the butt."

"So are you. It makes you a perfect couple."

"Go to hell, L.J.," Jake said.

Laura Jane grinned. "Just don't make the mistake of sleeping with her. Not a smart idea."

"I have no intention of touching her," he snapped. "And exactly why would it be a bad idea?"

"Because sex always complicates matters. And you, my dear boy, are not the love 'em and leave 'em type, even though you wish you were. So unless you want to spend the rest of your life with Molly Ferrell, I'd keep the relationship with her platonic. Distract her with enough stories to keep her convinced and then get her out of town before she finds out stuff you don't want her to know."

"Why don't you be the one to distract her?" Jake muttered.

"Because I don't have as strong a reason to keep the truth away from her. What's the problem, Jake? Afraid you can't resist her?"

"I can resist her just fine," he said in a cool, controlled voice. "She's not my type."

Laura Jane just laughed.

CHAPTER THREE

After seven days in Hidden Harbor, Molly was no longer so optimistic. Jake had proven true to his word, shadowing her wherever she went, and even if someone had felt like talking to her they'd take one look at Jake and clam up.

Even Laura Jane Twitchell was proving to be maddeningly elusive, and her mother-in-law was no help, either. By the time the first week was over Molly was almost ready to give up.

No one seemed to have any idea where Michael O'Flannery had lived. No one seemed to remember anything about him, but since they seemed to know every blessed thing about a newcomer like her, Molly found she couldn't quite believe their sudden amnesia.

Jake was the worst of all. She wouldn't have minded if he'd just been grumpy. But every now and then she caught him watching her when he thought she wouldn't notice, and there was an odd, almost distracted look about him. She couldn't decide whether it was intense dislike or confusion or both.

On her side, it was even worse. She dreamed about him. Not about Michael O'Flannery with her secret fantasies of a Byronic demon lover. No, it was Jake sneaking into her dreams, her bed, when she least expected it. And when she woke up, panting, sweating, trembling, it was Jake's face she pictured.

Of course, she'd have a hell of a time picturing Michael O'Flannery. At least she knew Jake was undeniably, unfortunately gorgeous in a bad-tempered, rough-hewn sort of way. And he was around almost every waking minute. It was entirely natural that her subconscious was reacting this way. Wasn't it?

She decided to give a little more time. Maybe today would be the day that Laura Jane would get a minute away from her family and her job and finally give her some of the answers she was looking for. Maybe today Jake would finally find something better to do than haunt her like the ghost of Christmas Past.

She woke a little after six, as usual, and her tiny room on the second floor of the inn was dark and chilly. Mrs. Twitchell would still be sound asleep, the place would be deserted until after eight and Molly needed coffee, badly. It was barely light when she got to the empty kitchen, and she was trying to decide whether she should go back and put on something warmer than her flannel nightgown when she smelled the coffee.

Her little moan of longing was instinctive, but it was enough to make the man in the shadows jump. She knew who it was before he moved into the light. Her self-appointed nemesis.

"Coffee's on the stove," he said.

She looked at it warily. "Rat poison?"

"French roast."

She moaned again, and Jake shifted uncomfortably. For the moment he wasn't scowling at her, and she realized why he bothered her. He was, in fact, absolutely gorgeous, from his dark blue eyes to his strong nose to his oddly sweet-looking mouth. Tall and lanky, with good shoulders and narrow hips, he was the epitome of what she found attractive. No wonder he bothered her. It was always unsettling to have a gorgeous man dislike you for no discernible reason.

Except that the reason was easily discerned. "Is this a truce?" she said, moving to the cupboards in search of a mug.

He moved past her, reaching over her head, too close. "They're here," he said, handing her a hand-thrown pottery mug.

She looked up at him, startled. Way too close. If he was trying to intimidate her with his sheer size then he was doing a good job of it. Except that intimidation wasn't the first thing on her mind.

She backed away from him, only slightly nervous, and his faint smile wasn't reassuring. "Stop looking at me like I'm some kind of axe murderer," he said. "I'm trying to be pleasant."

"Why?"

"Because I finally figured you aren't the type who'll give up easily, and trying to keep you away just makes you more curious. So I'm ready to cooperate. The whole town is. Ask any questions you want."

She stared at him uncertainly, the empty coffee mug dangling in her hand. "What made you change your mind?"

He took the mug and poured her a cup of coffee from the battered pot. "Because we're making you even more suspicious by not cooperating. Next thing I know, you'll decide Michael was murdered and start looking for suspects."

"Was he?" She took a sip. It was as good

as it smelled, a rare feat indeed, and she moaned with pleasure.

"Stop that!" Jake said sharply.

"You told me I could ask questions."

"Ask any questions you want. Just stop moaning and groaning over the coffee. It's not that orgasmic."

Molly jerked, startled. Normally the word wouldn't have bothered her in the slightest, but for some reason, in that dawn-lit kitchen it felt disturbingly erotic.

"Sorry," she muttered, grateful that the light was dim. "I don't tend to think of coffee in those terms."

He leaned against the counter, watching her. "So tell me what you want to know about Michael O'Flannery, and I'll do my best to help you."

She took another sip. She wasn't ready to trust his sudden helpfulness, but she was willing to take any advantage she could find, no matter what his motives. "I want to know everything. I want to know what he loved and what he hated, where he slept, where he died, why he killed himself, what happened to his family . . ."

"Damn!" Jake said in disgust. "You don't leave the poor kid any privacy, do you? If you want to know why he killed himself why don't you read a transcript of his sui-

cide note. I'm sure you can find it somewhere — it's public property."

"As a matter of fact, it's not," she said.
"It's mine."

"What?"

"I bought the original at auction a few
years ago. I have it with me."

He stared at her for a long moment.
"You're a sick woman."

"It's my area of expertise!" she protested, stung. "I'm writing a book about
O'Flannery — I'd buy anything that had to
do with him and his life if I could afford it."

"Sure," he said. Sarcasm wasn't a pretty
thing. "And you carry it with you? I bet
you sleep with it at night."

"Don't be ridiculous! I don't know
where you got the idea that my interest in
Michael O'Flannery is anything more than
academic . . ."

"You're fixated on a dead man," Jake
said, pushing away from the counter. Unfortunately she chose that moment to
move, and she bumped into him.

A small sort of bump, flesh and bone
against flesh and bone, an oddly seductive
brush of bodies. She jumped back nervously, but not so fast that she didn't see
the fleeting, contemplative expression on
his face. It made her uneasy.

"That would be pretty much a waste of time, now wouldn't it?" she said in a deceptively cool voice. "I'm much too practical to spend my life mooning over a dead poet."

"If you say so. You're not the first, you know. In the years after he killed himself all sorts of women showed up to weep at his grave and toss flowers into the ocean. Down at Binnie's we kept a running score. But they dwindled eventually, and we haven't seen one in a couple of years until you showed up. Why can't you let the dead rest in peace?"

"What makes you think he's resting in peace? He killed himself, remember?"

"Looking for that peace he couldn't find on earth."

"You knew him, didn't you?"

"It's a small town. Everyone knows everyone."

"You must be about his age," she said shrewdly. "How old are you?"

"Forty-five," he said without a blink. "How old are you?"

"None of your business. Almost thirty." She wasn't quite sure why she told him.

"Too young for me," he said.

"I beg your pardon?"

"And too old for O'Flannery. He was

just a kid when he died. A moping testos-terone bomb drunk on tragedy and the beauty of words. He would have loved his legend."

"Then why do you have a problem with me contributing to it? He's almost been forgotten over the last few years."

"Maybe it's better that way. Maybe it's about time to let him go."

"Have you ever read his stuff?" Molly demanded. "It's absolutely wonderful — it makes me weep it's so beautiful. How could you want his words forgotten?"

"Jesus!" Jake said, clearly disgusted.

"Who knows what he could have accom-plished if he'd lived?"

"I'll tell you what he would have accom-plished. He would have written another dozen obscure novels, each one more de-rivative, he would have put out a collection or two of poetry and then he would have spent the rest of his life at an Ivy League college teaching star-struck undergraduates the wonders of self-indulgent prose."

Molly stared at him in shock. "Why do you think that?"

"Because I knew him all his short life. He was a pain in the butt, too smart and too sensitive for his own good, and people like that don't last long in the real world."

Something wasn't right. What in the world did a carpenter know about O'Flannery's future? What in the world did a carpenter know about anything?

A lot, apparently.

"Look," he said in a long-suffering voice. "I'll help you find out what you need to know. I'll show you where he lived, answer your questions, whatever you want. But when you're finished I want you to leave."

"Why?"

"Because you don't belong here. O'Flannery's gone — there's nothing left for you here."

This was a strangely intimate conversation to be having with a man she didn't know. But then, after a week of his almost constant presence, she was almost beginning to feel comfortable with him. "I'll leave," she said. "When I find out what I need to know."

He didn't look satisfied, but there wasn't anything he could do about it, so he nodded. "What are we going to do today?" He leaned against the wooden counter, crossing his arms over his chest. He was wearing an old flannel shirt, faded from a thousand washings, and it looked very soft. The kind of thing Molly liked to sleep in — there was nothing better than well-aged cotton flannel. And why was she thinking about beds again? Every time the damned man was around her mind went out the window.

"Don't you have to work?"

He shrugged. "I can take the day off when I want to — one of the benefits of being self-employed. Anyway, I'm motivated to help you finish up. No need for you to linger in Hidden Harbor any longer than you have to. Winter's coming, and you've never felt how cold it can get until you've spent a winter on the ocean."

"What makes you think I haven't? And I wasn't planning to stay all winter."

"Snow comes early around here. So, unless you get a move on, you will be."

Still trying to get rid of her. His labored affability hadn't lasted long, though he was trying his damnedest, she thought. Well, two could play that game. She wasn't going to leave a moment sooner than she was ready to, but if Jake was willing to answer questions and help her, then she had every intention of taking advantage of it. She drained her coffee and smiled innocently at him.

"I'd like to see where he lived first."

"I can do that."

"Do you know the current owners?

Would they let me inside?"

"There are no current owners — the place has been closed up for years."

"Do you know where I can get a key?"

He seemed to be turning something over in his head. Finally he nodded. "I've got one. I suppose I can let you inside, though you aren't going to find anything of interest. He's been dead a long time."

"You didn't like him very much, did you?"

"Back then, no. But I've made my peace with him. Most teenage boys are self-conscious pains in the butt."

"I imagine you were, too," she pointed out in her sweetest voice.

"And still am, you're no doubt thinking." He didn't seem bothered by the notion. "I'll take you out to Crab Tree Road and show you the O'Flannery place. I'll even make Binnie be halfway pleasant to you, though that's a tall order. She used to be in love with O'Flannery and she's protective of his memory."

"So's the entire town."

Jake shrugged. "Maybe they feel guilty."

"Do they have reason to?"

"No."

"Do you have a reason to?"

"Maybe." He started toward the door,

effectively ending the subject. He paused, looking back at her. "When do you want to go?"

"What's wrong with now?" It was full light by now, and the coffee had only added to her restlessness.

"You might want to get dressed first," he said.

She looked down at herself with a start of surprise. She hadn't even realized she was still wearing the voluminous flannel nightgown she'd owned for more than five years, the fabric as soft as the shirt Jake was wearing. She could feel the color flood her face, but she simply squared her shoulders and met his ironic gaze. "I intended to," she said with a lack of concern that would have fooled most men.

Not Jake. "That's probably a good thing. You haven't been to New England before, have you?"

She wasn't going to like this, she thought. Suddenly she felt exposed beneath the yards of soft fabric, and for the first time she realized her bare feet were cold. "Why do you ask?" she said warily.

"Men in Maine find flannel nightgowns to be the sexual equivalent of lacy lingerie. One look at a woman in a flannel nightie can turn a normal, repressed New England male into a sex-obsessed love slave. They'll be following you around like a pack of dogs after a bitch in heat."

"You have a lovely way of putting things," she said sweetly. "At least you're immune to my siren charms."

His eyes met hers, and time seemed to stop. She caught her breath, unable to move, as she looked at him across the shadowy room. The moment stretched and grew, till she could feel the pounding of her heart, the strange knot in her stomach, and her mouth went dry.

"You'd be surprised," he said, opening the door. "I'll be back at nine." And he shut the door behind him.

She let out her breath in a whoosh. She was hot and cold at the same time. How the hell could she have stood there in nightgown, arguing with the man, and not realize how provocative she was? Well, who would have thought an old granny night-gown would be provocative?

Or maybe he was just trying to rattle her again. Make her so uncomfortable she forgot what she came for and got the hell out of here.

She wasn't going anywhere. He could try to intimidate her as much as he wanted to, but she wasn't falling for it. She wasn't going to let go of Michael O'Flannery until she was good and ready to.

No matter how tempting his old friend Jake was.

Damn, Jake thought as he strode down the empty streets toward Binnie's. Hell and damnation. The longer that woman stayed in town the worse trouble he was in. For some unfathomable reason she had the ability to get to him as few else could.

He could chalk it up to simple libido. He'd been in Hidden Harbor for so long that he already knew every available female. There'd been the occasional summer visitor who'd caught his eye, but he'd always done his best to keep his emotional distance, and they left before things got difficult.

It was harder with Molly, though he wasn't sure why. She got under his skin, like an itch, and he was determined not to scratch it. She was so pathetically in love with the idea of Michael O'Flannery that he should have been disgusted. She didn't even know what he looked like, and yet she was positively lovelorn. Carrying his suicide note around with her, for God's sake! What the hell was wrong with the woman? Couldn't she find someone alive and available to vent her romantic longings on?

He could make her forget Michael. It was a dangerous, deeply seductive notion. He could strip the clothes off Molly Ferrell's body and drive all thoughts of dead poets straight out of her mind as he drove his body —

Damn. He had to stop thinking this way. So what if for some in-explicable reason he found her hot? So what if her pathetic crush on Michael O'Flannery turned him on rather than disgusted him. So what?

He needed a dose of Binnie's attitude to set him straight. Women like Molly Ferrell were no good for him. No, scratch that. Molly Ferrell was no good for him.

He had strong doubts that there was anyone like her. And anyone as dangerous to his carefully constructed life.

He'd get rid of her. Today if he had to. By fair means or foul. Because the longer she stayed, the harder it became. And sooner or later she was going to find out the truth.

That he and he alone was responsible for the end of Michael O'Flannery.

CHAPTER FOUR

By nine o'clock the town of Hidden Harbor was in full swing. Mrs. Twitchell had already gone out on her daily shopping trip, the stores were open, the fishing boats had left the harbor hours before. And Jake stood outside the old inn, waiting for her, leaning against a large, rusty truck that had clearly seen better days.

"I'll drive," he said.

"I don't think so. I prefer my independence," Molly said. "I'll follow in my car."

He shrugged. "Suit yourself. The road's pretty rough and you don't have four-wheel drive."

He was trying to intimidate her, and she wasn't having any of it. "I'm sure I'll be fine. We have rough roads in Michigan, as well."

"Is that where you're from? You don't sound like a flatlander."

"Not originally. I grew up in Rhode Island, right on the ocean. It's been years since I've lived by the water." She tried to ignore the faintly plaintive note that had crept into her voice.

Jake shrugged. "Guess it's not in your blood. Most of the people around here find that once they live by the ocean there's no way they can live inland. They always come back to the sea. Some sort of primeval thing, I expect. You must have missed out on the gene."

She didn't bother denying it. She only wished it were true. The longer she stayed by the ocean, the more days she spent in that old-fashioned room overlooking the water, the harder it was to face going back to the broad flat spaces of Michigan, no matter how big the lakes were.

"That what you're wearing?" he demanded.

She looked down at her clothes. She had on her oldest pair of jeans and a long sleeve T-shirt. "What's wrong with it? At least I changed out of my nightgown. Don't tell me men around here get their passions inflamed by old jeans."

"Depends who's wearing them."

"Cut the crusty Yankee bit, will you?" she said irritably. "You can almost carry it off, but no one on earth is that rustic."

She half expected him to walk away, leaving her. Their truce was still on new and shaky ground, and she was a fool to risk alienating him. She waited for him to turn that fearsome glower on her.

His laugh was absolutely shocking in the morning air. It wasn't much of one, to be sure, just a dry chuckle of genuine amusement. "It fools the tourists," he said in a more amiable voice.

"I'm not so easy to trick."

"Now that remains to be seen. You better get a sweatshirt or a jacket or something. It's going to be cold out there near Claussen's Cove."

"I'll be fine. I don't get cold easily. I tend to have more of a problem with too much heat."

"Oh, really?" His tone was dulcet, and it was probably her own imagination that caught the sexual innuendo. And then she looked into his deliberately blank eyes and knew it wasn't her imagination after all.

The calm way he was looking down at her made her acutely uncomfortable. "Shouldn't we get going?" she said finally.

"What's your hurry? Michael O'Flannery isn't going anywhere. The house hasn't changed since it was closed up ten years ago." But he moved anyway, walking away from her and climbing into the truck.

The man could move, she had to admit that much. It wasn't so much a feline

54

grace, but there was something oddly powerful and yet graceful with all that carefully controlled strength churning inside him. If you could discount his gruff personality he was quite . . . nice.

But you couldn't discount it. At least, she couldn't, not when that attitude was so often directed at her.

"You coming?" His voice interrupted her thoughts.

The breeze had picked up, and she could feel just a trace of chill in the air. Nothing on earth, not even a raging blizzard, would make her go up to her room and get a jacket, not after he told her to. At least they were going to be indoors.

He was right about the roads, or lack thereof. The deep ruts had once been mud, now hardened into place in a series of craters and canyons that Molly couldn't even begin to straddle. With each bump and bounce she mentally took another month off the life of her exhaust system, which was already living on borrowed time. But at least she wasn't trapped in the cab of Jake's battered old truck. She didn't want to be anywhere near him. And she wasn't sure why.

Lord, she never lied to herself! Why was she starting now? She knew perfectly well why she didn't want to be cooped up with him, why she got restless and edgy and hostile whenever he turned his attention on her. She may be madly, deeply, romantically in love with the ghost of Michael O'Flannery and his lost, glorious words. But she had an undeniable case of the hots for Michael's cantankerous friend Jake.

It didn't make sense — she preferred men with a certain amount of savoir faire, of charm and sophistication. Jake was rough, sarcastic and totally devoid of charm. Well, maybe not totally. He knew just how to handle Marjorie Twitchell, and his gentle care of Davy was touching. He even radiated a certain charm with the women at Binnie's.

As far as she could see, she was the only one who wasn't deemed worthy of it. Screw him, she thought, and pushed her foot harder on the gas. She was rewarded with the worst pothole yet, and she cursed. Jake was ahead of her, his huge truck navigating the rough terrain like it was a newly paved highway. She could see his long dark hair behind the mud-splashed rear window of the cab. She'd always had a weakness for long hair, and never yet had a boyfriend who wore his any way but short.

She was almost thirty — too old for boyfriends. Too old to be having sexual fantasies about Jake. She was much better off thinking about Michael O'Flannery. At least in his case she wouldn't be in any kind of danger of going to bed with him. He could stay in her dreams, doomed and tragic and perfect.

It was taking them a hell of a long time to find Crab Tree Lane, and they drove over one horrific rut that Molly was certain she'd hit before, the bottom of her Honda scraping painfully on the hard surface. He was probably taking her the most circuitous, roundabout route he could think of, just to ensure she couldn't find her way back here on her own. He needn't have worried — she was generally hopeless when it came to directions. She'd taken a wrong turn a total of seven times on the trip from Michigan to Maine. If she tried to get back here on her own, even if he'd gone the most direct way, she probably would have ended up at the Pacific Ocean.

The O'Flannery house was even more depressing than she'd expected. It was three-stories tall, narrow, with broken, peeling clapboards. Some of the windows were boarded over, the shutters nailed tight, though she was grateful that at least a few of them seemed intact. The day was cool and overcast, and she expected that any electricity the old wreck had ever boasted had been turned off long ago.

Jake had already parked the truck, so she pulled up beside him and turned off the engine. He was nowhere to be seen, and she approached the house warily, half expecting him to appear out of nowhere.

She stopped in front of the broad, cracked front steps and looked out at the sagging porch that stretched across the front of the house. If Michael sat there, he would have faced town, not the glorious freedom of the ocean.

This is where he lived, she told herself. Michael O'Flannery had lived almost all of his twenty short years in this bleak, depressing house, and it was here that he'd written his final, epic poem, scribbled a suicide note and walked out into nothingness with a shotgun in his hand.

Would she feel him? Smell him? Could she touch the walls and sense his presence over those long years? Would his bed still be there? And could she lie down on it and close her eyes, just for a moment, without Jake catching her? Or did she want him to catch her?

A dark figure loomed out of the shadows on the porch, taking her by surprise. It was

Davy, his face twisted into an angry glare, his big body menacing. "What are you doing here?" he shouted at her. "You aren't supposed to know about this place. We don't want you here — didn't Jake tell you that? Go away. Go back to where you came from."

She didn't move, frozen. Where the hell was Jake? Everyone kept insisting that Davy was harmless, but right at that moment Molly was far from convinced. He'd decided to hate her, there was no doubt about that, and she hadn't been able to figure out why. Unless it was the same reason most of Hidden Harbor seemed to despise her. "Hi, Davy," she said in a soft, calm voice. "Jake brought me out here. He's around someplace."

"No, he didn't," he said flatly. "He wouldn't do that. Jake says we have to protect Michael, no matter what. We can't let you ruin everything. I won't let it happen."

"What would I ruin?" she asked, confused. It hadn't taken long for Davy to decide that she was the epitome of evil. One moment she was a pretty lady, in the next, a menace to society. Unfortunately his later reaction had been the one that stayed.

"You have to stop asking questions!" He moved to the top of the stairs, glaring down at her, and she realized he was holding something behind his back. Something big. A little shiver of nervousness slid down her spine.

"Don't you think we should find Jake, Davy? He'll want to see you, don't you think? Maybe he went around the back of the house to unlock it . . ."

Davy shook his head, descending the first step. "He wouldn't do that. I think he brought you here on purpose, so I could take care of things for him. He can't drive you away, but I can. No one would bother with me because I'm not right. That's what people tell me. They wanted to put me in the hospital over in Sanford, but Jake wouldn't let them. He told them I wouldn't hurt a fly. And I wouldn't."

"Of course you wouldn't," Molly said soothingly. "You know, it's getting sort of chilly. I think I'll just go to my car and find a sweater." And get inside and lock the doors, she thought nervously.

"Stay where you are!" Davy descended another step, and Molly got a good look at what he was holding behind his back. It wasn't reassuring.

She could always assume the old shotgun wasn't loaded. That it didn't work. That Davy wouldn't even know how to use the thing, or if he did he was only bluffing. Her thoughts didn't help. She stood there, frozen, waiting to see whether he'd pull that gun from behind his back and aim it at her. And to see whether Jake was going to show up in time to rescue her, or whether this was what he'd always had in mind.

The sky had grown darker still, the ominous shadows only increasing her unease. Surely she couldn't be in that much danger. She didn't want to die out here in the middle of nowhere on such a dark, windswept day.

Another step, and Davy grew closer still. She could run for it, but she didn't fancy being shot in the back while she tried to escape. If she could just calm Davy down . . .

"Why did you want to come here for?" Davy demanded fretfully. "Why do all you people come and cause trouble?"

"I'm not . . ."

"Don't lie to me!" Davy's voice rose in an agitated shriek. "You think you can fool me but you can't. You just want to come and mix everything up, and I can't let you do that."

"Davy!" Jake had come up behind her, and he moved in front of her, blocking her with his tall body. "What are you doing out here?"

The menace vanished. "Hi, Jake," he said, dropping the old shotgun on the ground. "I wasn't doing anything."

Jake crossed the overgrown yard and picked up the old gun. "Where did you get this, Davy?"

Davy shifted guiltily. "It wasn't loaded."

"That doesn't matter. You know you're not supposed to touch guns. You know you're not supposed to hurt anyone. Why would you want to hurt Molly? She's nice, remember? She's a pretty lady."

"You know," Davy said in a sullen voice.

"Get in the truck, Davy. I'll take you back into town."

"What about her?" Davy jerked his head in Molly's direction. "You don't want her snooping . . ."

"I brought her out here, Davy," he said in a patient voice. "It's all right."

"But we can't let her find out."

"Get in the truck," he said again. "Everything will be fine."

Without another word Davy went, skirting around Molly as if she carried the plague. Jake set the shotgun against the stairs and followed him, pausing for a moment by Molly. "Are you all right? Did he scare you?"

He sounded genuinely concerned. "I'm fine," she said. He didn't have to know that her knees were shaking. "You take him home."

"He wouldn't have hurt you, you know."

She didn't know any such thing, but she nodded. "I'm fine," she repeated. "I'll just head back to the inn and we can do this later."

The fleeting look of frustration told her all she needed to know about their round-about route. "I think you might have trouble finding your way. I've unlocked the house — why don't you go in and have a look around while I take Davy home?"

That was the last thing she expected. "You trust me?"

"Trust doesn't enter into it. There's nothing to find." His slow smile should have annoyed her. Instead she felt that answering tug in the pit of her stomach. "Take your time, rummage through drawers and closets, snoop to your heart's content. It shouldn't take me more than an hour to get Davy settled and then I'll be back and you can pump me for all the information you want."

An unfortunate choice of words on his part, but she didn't let herself react. She stood in the yard, watching him as he drove away, then she headed for the wide front steps of the house.

The gun was still lying there. She probably ought to pick it up and carry it into the empty house, but she didn't want to touch it. It was old, even rusty, and she hated guns. From what she'd read, she guessed it was very much like the one that Michael O'Flannery had carried into the woods to end his life.

The door squeaked when she pushed it open, and the musty smell of the place spilled out over her. It was cold and damp when she stepped inside, but she closed the door behind her and took a deep breath.

Jake was right — there was nothing to find. Just a bunch of sagging furniture, worn rugs and the scent of despair lingering on the air. The house was smaller than it looked outside. There were four rooms on each floor. Kitchen, living room, dining room and parlor on the first, all with the same depressing wallpaper.

And four bedrooms on the second floor.

It was easy enough to tell which one had been Michael's, simply by process of elimination. It was the only room that still held something other than furniture. An old bookcase stood against one wall, and there were books stacked everywhere — on the shelves, on the floor, even a couple on the narrow, sagging iron bed.

She picked up the ones from the bed. The mattress was covered with a faded, ugly brown bedspread. It must have been O'Flannery's. He must have stretched out on that tiny bed and looked toward the sea, lost in dreams.

She dumped the books on the old desk, then looked back at the bed, trying to picture him stretched out on the battered surface. All she could see was Jake.

He had been right — there was nothing left to find in this sad, empty building. Nothing to do but sit and wait for Jake to return. Sit in this cold, quiet house, shivering.

She wasn't a complete masochist. She pulled the old coverlet from the bed, wrapping it around her shoulders for warmth, and she sat on the bed, looking out at the sea in the distance. She could feel Michael there, all around her, in the fabric of the coverlet, in the dead air, in the floor beneath her feet.

This had been his bed, she thought. And she looked down at the plain horsehair mattress and froze.

It was an ordinary enough mattress, covered with plain blue ticking. And blood, the twenty-year-old stains of a life bleeding away.

Jake was coming up the front steps when she ran out of the house, the coverlet still around her shoulders. He caught her as she almost barreled into him, his hands hard and strong and somehow reassuring on her upper arms, holding her still.

"What's wrong? You look like you've seen a ghost. Did Michael's spirit decide to pop out at you?"

"Blood," was all she could say. She'd been in such a panic she was breathless. "I know where he died."

"Do you?"

"In bed. He killed himself in bed, and someone, maybe you, covered it up. There's blood all over the mattress, dried blood. But why would you . . . ?"

"He didn't die in bed, Molly," Jake said with surprising patience.

"Then where did all that blood come from? And don't tell me it was a nosebleed or a little cut — I won't believe you. I don't know why I believe you anyway, since you have no reason to tell me the truth and every reason to want me gone."

"I do, don't I?" he said, half to himself. "I assume you're talking about the mattress in the back room? The one that used to be covered by this bedspread?" He tugged at the coverlet still clutched around her shoulders. "As a matter of fact, it wasn't a little cut, it was a big one. Michael tried to kill himself in a drunken stupor a year before he died. He slashed his wrists, but someone found him in time, took him to the hospital and patched him up, good as new for one more year."

"Who found him? Did you?"

"Not me. As a matter of fact, it was Davy. That's partly why he feels so protective about Michael's memory. Ever since he saved his life he feels responsible for it. Half the time he thinks that Michael isn't dead. He's just hiding somewhere."

"Is he?"

He stepped back from her, dropping his hands. "Don't be ridiculous."

"Well, everyone's going out of their way to hide something, and it has to do with O'Flannery's death. Did someone kill him? Did Davy kill him? Did you?"

"You should be writing thrillers. Michael's dead and gone, but it's by his own hand and no one else's. This town doesn't need you to start rumors. . . ."

"I'm not going to start rumors. I just want to know the truth."

He closed his eyes in frustration, then glared at her. "The truth is a matter of opinion. Michael is gone forever. That's all you need to know."

She looked up at him, tense and frustrated. He was lying to her and they both knew it. "I'm going home," she said abruptly.

"It's about time."

"I mean I'm going back to the inn. I'm not leaving this town. You can't drive me away, either by threatening me or by being nice. There's nothing you can do to make me leave here before I'm good and ready to."

"You think so?" he said. And before she had any idea what he had in mind he pulled her into his arms and kissed her.

Jake had a number of good, believable reasons for kissing Molly Ferrell. At any other day and time he could have listed them with cool detachment, and he could have convinced anyone, maybe even himself.

But not with her body pressed up against his, not with her mouth beneath his, not with the heat and need that had suddenly flared up out of nowhere.

The bedspread fell to the ground around

her, and she put her hands against his chest, maybe to push him away, but it didn't matter, because she opened her mouth to his, letting him inside, and the quiet sound in the back of her throat was even more orgasmic than her reaction to coffee. He knew he was getting hard, almost immediately, and he knew he should back away from her, before things got out of control.

Why was he kissing her? To scare her into leaving, to distract her from what she was looking for, to make her think twice about going off into the middle of nowhere with a strange man?

Hell, no, he was kissing her because he wanted to. Because he couldn't stop thinking about her eyes, her mouth, her breasts, her legs, hadn't been able to since the day she arrived, unwanted, in Hidden Harbor.

This morning he'd just about hauled her onto the kitchen table and taken her then and there. That old flannel nightgown of hers was so worn, so thin, he could see the darkness of her nipples beneath the cloth. And he'd had to stand there, keeping his eyes on her face, keeping the counter between them, clutching his coffee to stop himself from jumping her. So he'd spent all that time staring at her mouth, her soft, luscious mouth, and look where it got him. In real, deep trouble.

And he didn't care. He lifted his head to look down at her, catching his breath. Her eyes were closed, and he could feel her trembling in his arms, and he didn't know whether it was cold or fear or something else. Her eyes fluttered open, and she looked up at him, confused, aroused, dazed.

There was only one thing he could do. "You want to go in and try out Michael's mattress?" he said, deliberately crude.

She pushed him away with a choked sound, and now he was the one who was cold.

CHAPTER FIVE

Common sense had nothing to do with it, only instinct. Molly shoved him away, hard, and started for her car, when what she really wanted to do was hold on to him.

Her foot got caught in the discarded bedspread, and she went sprawling in the dirt, her ankle twisting, her knee slamming against something hard and unforgiving. Her reaction was short, sharp and profane.

"If that's supposed to impress me, you've got a long way to go," Jake said, as if he hadn't just been kissing her, as if she hadn't just felt the deep, burning need that had ignited between them. He reached down and pulled her to her feet with no more tenderness than if he were picking up a sack of potatoes.

A sack of potatoes that refused to be held. "Let go of me," Molly said sharply, and pulled away. She knew she couldn't walk, at least not immediately, so she simply sat down on the ground, on the offending bedspread, and took a deep breath.

She had a weak ankle, and it had a stupid tendency to twist beneath her on occasion. All she needed to do was ice and elevate it and she'd be fine by tomorrow, but in the meantime she was stuck in the middle of nowhere with a man she didn't trust. To top it off, whatever she'd landed on had managed to rip her favorite pair of old jeans, and her knee was scraped and bleeding beneath the torn fabric.

She swore again, finding a better word this time. Jake squatted down in front of her, looking at her bloody knee. "That looks nasty," he said.

"That's not very helpful! And it looks worse than it feels," she said, only a little white lie.

"Then why can't you walk?"

"I twisted my ankle."

He swore then, a much more impressive curse. "Obviously I'll have to get you home."

"If you could just help me to my car I can drive myself . . ."

"With a sprained ankle? With a stick shift? I don't think so."

"It's not sprained," she protested. "It'll be fine by tomorrow."

He simply looked at her with his dark blue eyes, and there was no way she could tell what he was thinking. Why had he kissed her? Why had he stopped?

"Suit yourself," he said finally, rising. He held out a hand to help her up, and Molly gritted her teeth, determined not to show pain.

She managed to take two steps on her own before he came up behind her, slid his arm around her waist and scooped her up in his arms. It was a dizzying sensation. "What the hell are you doing?" she demanded, breathless.

"Damned if I know," he muttered, carrying her over to the truck. He managed to open the passenger door while he still held her, and dumped her inside on the seat with an expected lack of ceremony.

She didn't bother trying to get out. She already knew she wouldn't get far until her ankle improved, and having him chase after her would be undignified. Not to mention what might happen when he caught her.

She watched as he headed back to the abandoned house, picking up the old coverlet and the abandoned gun and tossing them inside the front door before he locked it.

The truck was a full-size one with a roomy cab, but the moment he climbed in, it felt as cramped as a sports car.

He pulled away from the house. "Put your seat belt on," he said. "And don't bleed all over my truck."

"Then give me something to use as a bandage. Where the hell are we going?" she demanded as he started driving farther out on the point, toward the ocean.

"Since I don't seem to be able to get rid of you, I thought I'd dump you over a cliff. O'Flannery's parents died that way, you know. His father was drunk as always, his mother was raging, and he took a wrong turn and their car went off the road and into the ocean. I kind of thought you might like to die in the same spot."

"What?" she gasped, looking at him in horror.

He spared a glance at her, that half smile playing around his mouth. "Just kidding."

"You're a sick bastard," she said shakily.

"Takes one to know one," he responded. "I don't carry suicide notes around with me or fall in love with dead people. As a matter of fact . . . I'm driving you to my place to bandage you up and see whether you need stitches, and then I'll take you either to the hospital or back to the inn. Where you'll no doubt have a good night's sleep and get back to snooping in the morning instead of going home like you ought to."

"Why don't you drive me straight to town? Since you're so worried about me bleeding all over your truck?"

"Because I live half a mile away and Hidden Harbor is four miles on rough roads. You're safe with me, Molly. I wouldn't touch you with a ten-foot pole."

"So I noticed."

He glanced at her again, but she ignored him, staring out the window at the landscape beyond. They were heading out toward the ocean, and the pine trees grew tall around the narrow, rutted road, strong enough to withstand the battering of the ocean winds. There were cliffs off to the right, and on the left side the land sloped gradually down to the sea.

"I don't see any houses," she said.

"You're not supposed to see it. I like my privacy." He kept driving, and she indulged herself in looking at him.

"There's Ethan Frome resurfacing again," she said in a snotty voice.

"Hardly. Ethan Frome was willing to die for love. I'm much too pragmatic."

"To be in love, or to die for it?"

His dark blue eyes swept over her for a moment, then looked away. But he didn't answer.

"Were you telling me the truth?" she asked after a moment. Stupid question, when she doubted he'd ever told her the truth in the short time she'd known him.

The road ahead of them ended in a turn-around, and he pulled the car to a stop, shifting in his seat to look at her.

"About what?"

"About Michael's parents. I knew they died in a car accident when he was seventeen. Did they really go over the cliff?"

"They did."

"They aren't buried with their son. Why not?"

"They were good Catholics and got to be in the cemetery by St. Mary's. Michael, on the other hand, committed a mortal sin, so he had to settle for the lesser hell of a Protestant burial."

"But he wasn't buried. No one found his body. Did they?"

The silence in the truck grew. It wasn't even noon, and yet the day was growing ominously darker. The wind had picked up, and there was a sharp chill in the air. A chill that reached into the cab of the truck and into Molly's heart.

"No one found his body," Jake agreed after a moment. He glanced out the window. "Looks like the storm's coming sooner than they thought."

"What storm?" Molly demanded. "I didn't hear anything about a storm."

"That's because you're a flatlander who doesn't pay attention to the weather. There's a nor'easter coming up the coast, but it was supposed to go out to sea. Looks like it changed direction."

"Don't you think you better drive me into town, then? Before it hits?"

"We have plenty of time." He climbed out of the truck, leaving the keys in the ignition, and headed around to the passenger side.

"You forgot your keys," she said, reaching for them. "Someone might steal your truck."

"No one ever comes out here. Even in town I leave my keys in the truck. People don't steal around here."

"Must be nice," Molly muttered. He'd opened her door and was standing there, waiting for her, hands reaching for her. Hands that would touch her, when she found his touch . . . disturbing.

Hell, she was overreacting. If a man kissed her it was only natural that she be wary of him. Particularly when she hadn't been kissed in longer than she wanted to remember. It seemed like years. Robert had never been much for kissing.

"I can make it on my own," she said, starting to slide off the high seat. Of course he ignored her, putting his strong hands on her waist and lifting her down.

"Do I need to carry you?"

"You need to take me back to town. . . ." He swooped her up in his arms again. She was a good one hundred and twenty-five pounds, but he kicked the door shut and started down the narrow path beneath the twisted pines without even breaking a sweat.

She didn't know what she was expecting when his house came into view. Some kind of fisherman's shanty, or maybe a rusty mobile home. She'd forgotten he was a carpenter.

The building lay sprawled in front of them, a magical combination of angles and lines, glass and wood, mystical and pragmatic. The ocean, angry today with the approaching storm, was beyond the house, and on all sides the tall trees sheltered and half hid the building.

He wasn't waiting for her reaction, which was just as well. She didn't want to like his place, but she did. She didn't want to like him, but she did, far too much. And she was beginning to think that maybe he was right after all, and she should get herself the hell away from this town. Away from Hidden Harbor, with its ghosts and its temptations.

The house smelled like cinnamon and woodsmoke and cedar, and it was blessedly warm. She hadn't realized how cold she was until he dumped her on the sofa and stepped back.

He fit in this room, with the huge windows looking out onto the storm-tossed sea, the walls of bookcases and shabby, old furniture. The place was sloppy-male — with dishes and newspapers scattered about, and the old couch beneath her was possibly the most comfortable thing in the world.

He was watching her. Despite all the windows, the room was dark, and he switched on a light on the desk. He had an open laptop computer, and he shut the lid as he walked back to her, a casual gesture that she shouldn't have noticed.

"Take off your pants," he said.

"Yeah, sure."

"How am I supposed to clean up that mess on your knee if you don't? For that matter, you probably could do with an ace bandage on your ankle, and I don't think I can get to it with those jeans on."

"And what do you propose I wear while you're administering first aid?"

He shrugged. "I don't suppose you'd believe me if I told you you were safe from my lust-crazed advances."

"Oh, I'd believe you. I'm not an idiot. I know the only reason you kissed me was to try to get me out of town. For all I know you might be willing to make the ultimate sacrifice just to get rid of me. What are you grinning about?"

" 'The ultimate sacrifice,' " he repeated. "Yeah, I suppose I could bring myself to do it for a noble cause. Would it drive you out of town?"

Why the hell had she even brought up the subject of his kiss? Much less where it was leading. Her knee hurt like hell, her ankle was throbbing, but all she could think about was him. "Would what?" she said, stalling for time.

Big mistake. He crossed the room to lean over her, and she slid back on the couch, trying to get away from him, from his closeness, which was both intimidating and strangely, sweetly tempting. "Would sleeping with you get you out of town?"

She swallowed, trying to look fearless. "It depends on how bad you are at it."

He blinked. And then he laughed.

She liked his laugh. It was a deep chuckle, one that went well with the reluctant little half smile that took over when he wasn't fighting it. "You're a dangerous woman, Molly Ferrell," he said, moving back, out of reach. "I think I'm safer keeping my distance."

"In that case I'll take off my pants. Assuming you've got a quilt or something I can wrap around me while you perform triage."

"Behind you on the sofa. I'll go get the first-aid stuff."

It probably wasn't a good idea, she thought, shimmying out of her torn jeans. Then again, how aroused was he going to get at the sight of her bloody, scraped knee and swollen ankle? He wasn't going to take her home until he cleaned her up, and she really wanted to go home. Didn't she?

She wrapped the quilt around her waist, pulling it up to expose her knee. The bleeding had pretty much stopped, but even in the dim light it looked as if she'd gotten some dirt in there, and the wound was already closing up. He was right that she needed it taken care of right away. She didn't like it when he was right.

He came back into the room with an armful of ominous-looking supplies. "Lie down," he said.

"What is all this? Take off your pants, lie down. Don't you know the word *please?*" she said, irritable. Irritable because his order had sounded far too tempting.

"Would you please lie back on the sofa so I can take a look at your knee?" he said with thinly disguised patience.

"Is it going to hurt?"

"Most likely."

"You'll enjoy that," she accused him.

"Most likely. Are you going to lie down or are we going to keep talking?"

She lay back on the sofa, closing her eyes. And then opening them immediately as she felt him kneel down by her.

He wasn't looking at her, he was looking at her knee. She had good legs, when they weren't covered in blood. Nothing to be nervous about. And then she felt his hand on her calf and she jumped.

"Why are you so skittish?" he said, his deep, irascible voice a small comfort. He couldn't be thinking the same thing she was if he sounded so grumpy.

"Sorry," she muttered. "Go ahead." She turned to stare at the bookshelves, concentrating on the titles. He had the strangest collection of stuff. Michael O'Flannery's small body of work was easy enough to find, and she wondered whether they were autographed. They must be, since Jake had known him all his short, tragic life. There were books on birds and nature, art books and shelves of mysteries, including what appeared to be the entire collection of Sydney Carton's works. She glanced back at Jake. They had more in common than she realized, and the thought bothered her. It was a shame and a sin in the academic community to read genre fiction, and Molly kept her vice secret, even when it came to a writer as wonderful as Sydney Carton. Jake was the first person she'd met who seemed to share her passionate enthusiasm.

"You like mysteries?" she asked, her voice only slightly strained. He'd put one hand under her knee, his fingers splayed on her thigh, and she was having a little trouble concentrating. The pain was nothing compared to the feel of his hands on her leg.

"In books, not in real life," he said, following her gaze. "Not your cup of tea, of course."

"I love Sydney Carton."

He looked at her, startled. "Now that I find hard to believe."

"You must know how good he is, otherwise you wouldn't have all of his books."

Again that wry little half smile. "They're not bad for trashy paperbacks," he murmured.

"You're worse than my snotty colleagues."

"I doubt that. I'm sure you feel right at home with all those lofty academics."

"You're sure of a lot of things that you know absolutely nothing about," she said.

"You don't like teaching?"

"I love teaching. I just don't like the politics. The bureaucracy, the competition. I never get any time with the students — it's all spent on meetings and grant writing and backstabbing. Once I get tenure it'll probably be even worse."

"What did you think it would be like? High school?"

"I probably would have been a lot happier if it was."

"Then why don't you teach high school?"

"And waste my education?" she said, horrified.

"Seems to me it's more of a waste spending your life doing something you don't really like, when you could do something you cared about and help people at the same time."

His hands left her legs, and he sat back on his heels, watching her.

"Why would I be helping people?"

84

"Because most high school teachers are crap, but a good one changes lives."

"Maybe I don't want to change lives."

"Sure you do, Molly. You want to wade into people's lives and mess around with them and fix them, I can see it in your eyes. I'm sure you think that if you had just met Michael O'Flannery you would have saved him."

"I was eleven when he died. That's a little young for saving people," she said, trying to be caustic when that was exactly what she'd fantasized, and then she realized that he'd put his hand back on her legs, his fingers just brushing her skin with something that could almost be called a caress. "What are you doing?"

"You know what I'm doing," he said, sliding his hand up her thigh. "I'm trying to drive you away." His fingertips touched the edge of the quilt she had bunched around her. "Is it working?"

"Yes!" she said in a nervous little squeak.

"Then why aren't you running?"

"I hurt my ankle."

"Lucky me." He tugged at the quilt, and she held on tightly. "Are we going to have a tug of war? I'd win."

"You should take me back to the inn."

"I know I should. Do you want me to?"

Somehow one hand had slid up under the bunched-up quilt. He had wicked, clever hands, and before she knew what he was doing he'd slid his fingers beneath her panties, touching her.

"Yes," she said in a tiny yelp. And he touched her again, a little harder. "Please," she said.

His eyes were as hard as diamonds in the dimly lit room, and behind him she could see the storm coming down on them, the trees whipping in the wind, the crash of the waves on the rocky beach. And then she couldn't see anything at all, as his head blocked out the light and he kissed her.

CHAPTER SIX

He'd known this was going to happen the minute he set eyes on her. He'd taken one look at her across Marjorie Twitchell's kitchen and known exactly where it would lead. It didn't matter how hard he tried to avoid her, how bad an idea this was. He'd known he was going to be kissing her, his hands between her legs, and all the denial in the world wasn't going to stop it.

The second kiss was even better than the first. Tasting her mouth again was like coming home to something strange yet familiar, a place he wanted to go again and again. Her lips were soft, tentative, but she didn't resist. She tentatively touched his tongue with hers, and there was a sudden flash of light, followed by the crashing sound of thunder, and the room was plunged into darkness.

It didn't matter. Outside the house the storm hit with a wild, unexpected fury. Inside everything was heat.

"Don't do this," she said, sliding her

arms around his neck and pulling him down to her mouth. "This is a very bad idea."

"Yes," he said, and he picked her up in his arms, dropping the quilt on the floor. He wanted to push her up against the wall and take her there, he wanted to throw himself on top of her on the sofa. But if he was fool enough to do this, he was going to do it right.

He could feel the tension running through her body as he made his way through the darkness. She was shivering, but the house was warm, and he knew she was frightened.

"You should take me home." She kissed the side of his neck.

"Yes," he said.

"Where are you taking me?"

"To bed."

She didn't bother arguing, just buried her face against his shoulder as he carried her into the darkness. He put her down on the wide bed that he'd never shared with anyone, and began to strip off her clothes, the baggy white T-shirt, the flimsy under-wear, the bra that he wanted to rip off her. He didn't — she was scared enough. But not so scared that she didn't lie back on the bed, waiting for him.

They made love in silence, her only sound the small muffled cry when he pushed deep inside her. He stopped, afraid he'd hurt her, but she wrapped her legs around his hips, pulling him closer, and he felt the first shimmers of climax course through her body.

He wanted to make her come first, so he could concentrate on his own pleasure, but it didn't work out that way. It didn't take him long to figure out what she liked, the way she wanted him to move. It was easy enough to read the choking sound of her breathing, the sudden spasm in her body. But he hadn't expected her first, tentative orgasm to trigger his own, and he couldn't stop, couldn't hold back, as he felt her tighten around him with an anxious sort of wail. And then he was lost, buried in her, wrapped around her, holding her, as pure sensation swept over him, shaking him to pieces.

He caught his breath before she did. His heart was hammering against his ribs, but at least he could breathe. She was still gasping for air when he rolled over, taking her with him.

"Careful of your knee," was all he said.

"Forget my knee," she said, and leaned over to kiss him.

She was asleep in his arms when the lights came back on five hours later. It was no wonder she was exhausted — he'd done more in those five hours than he'd done in the last five years. And he wasn't finished.

She didn't wake up immediately, and he gave in to the rare indulgence of watching her while she slept. At some point she'd cried, maybe more than once. He could see the stain of tears on her cheeks. Her mouth was red, swollen from his, and there were whisker burns on her face and neck. And between her thighs.

If he'd known what was going to happen he would have shaved. He wanted to kiss her soft skin where his own had abraded it. He wanted to lick it. He wanted to bite it.

He was getting hard again, and he thought she'd probably reached her limit. He needed to think about something else, but that was a little difficult with a soft, naked woman in his arms.

Then he realized she was awake, staring up at him with troubled eyes. She was already regretting it, ready to run. Just as well, he thought. Maybe this time she really would leave town, and he could forget about her. Maybe.

She pulled away from him, and he let her go, reluctantly. They'd kicked the covers off the bed long ago, but she fished around and found the sheet, pulling it around her as she looked at him. He didn't have much of a chance to see her body before she covered up, but he already knew he liked it. Hell, he was obsessed by it. He would have liked to have made love in the light, but clearly the time had passed.

"This was a mistake," she said.

"Yeah?" he said. "Why?"

"I don't even know you. We don't like each other. I don't do things like this."

"You just did. And it doesn't matter whether we like each other or not. It goes beyond that."

"Don't be ridiculous," she said, clutching the sheet to her. "Do you think I'm in love with you? That I have some sort of adolescent crush on you and all you had to do was touch me and I melted?"

She was beginning to piss him off. "No, I think you have an obsession with Michael O'Flannery. You probably jumped me because you thought I was the closest thing left to him."

"I did not jump you! You jumped me."

"Let's say the jumping was mutual," he drawled, getting out of bed and reaching for his discarded jeans. "And don't tell me you didn't enjoy it. You may have been closing your eyes, pretending I was your precious Michael, but it was me inside you. Not some dead poet."

"Why are you so jealous of him? You really hate him, don't you?" she said. "What did he ever do to you?"

"Oh, no," he shot back. "I'm not going to give you more ammunition for your little tell-all."

"I told you, I'm writing about his work, not his life. What did Michael O'Flannery do to you to make you hate him so much? Because you do hate him, don't you?"

He crossed the room, so fast she couldn't duck out of the way, and knelt on the bed, looming over her. "He ruined my life."

She stared up at him. "Did you kill him?"

"What?"

"Don't look so innocent! The whole town acts guilty as sin, you in particular. Did you kill Michael O'Flannery?"

He didn't even hesitate; he was in an ugly mood. He wasn't quite sure what he'd expected from her, but it wasn't this suspicion. "As a matter of fact, I did."

She didn't move. Then suddenly she scrambled off the bed, the sheet still wrapped around her, and took off.

For a moment he thought she'd go sprawling on the hardwood floor, but she managed to hobble into the living room at a half run. She was going to have a difficult time finding her clothes; they were strewn all over the place, and he didn't even know where she'd put her jeans. He grabbed a T-shirt and followed her, scooping up her discarded clothes along the way.

She was sitting on the sofa, staring at the bookshelf. He dumped her clothes in her lap, then turned away. "I'll take you back to the inn now," he said.

"What if I call the police?"

"Habeas corpus, Molly. No body, no death." And he turned away from her before he gave in to temptation and touched her. Because he knew damned well she'd give in, as well, and touch him back, and things were already screwed up enough.

She dressed quickly, ignoring the pain in her knee and ankle, ignoring the tenderness in other, less-exposed parts of her body. She must be sicker than she thought. She'd just had the best sex of her entire life with a hostile stranger who admitted he murdered someone. She should be calling the police, and instead she was thinking of the last few hours and the feel of his skin against hers.

He was lying. He had to be. He couldn't have killed Michael O'Flannery. The people of Hidden Harbor wouldn't cover up such a crime, not unless O'Flannery himself was some kind of vicious monster — a child molester or worse — who had to be exterminated.

But O'Flannery was no such thing. He was just a poor, lost soul with a miraculous gift for words, and he'd died too young. At Jake's hands?

It was impossible. And yet there'd been no hesitation, no doubt when he said he'd killed him. And the hideous thing was, Molly believed him.

She stood up, trying to put a bit of weight on her bad ankle. It held, just barely, and she limped across the room to the desk. To the telephone. She needed to call the police before she could change her mind. It didn't matter whether they listened to her or not, she had to tell someone, soon. Or else she'd end up protecting him, hiding the truth because she'd made the incredibly stupid mistake of falling in love with him.

She really was an idiot, she thought, sitting down at the desk. Most of her life had been spent mooning over a dead writer, and now she'd simply shifted to his killer.

Next thing she knew she'd be writing love letters to inmates on death row.

How could he have done it? Why had he done it? To take a human life was something you couldn't go back from. It would haunt him, doom him, a chain around his neck like . . . like . . .

A sudden cold chill swept over her body. A chain around his neck, haunting him, like the ghost of Jacob Marley in *A Christmas Carol*. Jake Marley.

She shook her head. It was absurd, a crazy, weird coincidence. She turned to look out the windows, suddenly sick inside, when her eyes caught the wall of bookshelves. The row of paperback mysteries, brilliant, literary mysteries by one Sydney Carton. Another Dickens character.

She opened the computer in front of her, but she knew perfectly well what she'd find. Sydney Carton's latest work in progress.

"What are you doing?" He'd come back into the room, and she closed the lid of the laptop slowly.

She rose, and her ankle didn't buckle. Her anger was so strong it made her invincible. She limped across the room, straight toward him, and he didn't flinch, he just stood there watching her, an unreadable expression on his face.

She picked up his hand and turned it over. The scars were still there, barely visible, from his suicide attempt so long ago. At least he hadn't lied about that.

"You son of a bitch," she said softly. "You lying, deceitful bastard."

He didn't bother denying it. "What? I was supposed to tell you? Say, 'Welcome to Hidden Harbor and by the way, Michael O'Flannery isn't really dead, he just doesn't want to be bothered by people like you.' "

"Michael J. O'Flannery. Michael Jacob. I'm a stupid, gullible idiot," she said bitterly.

"Yes," he said. "But you're the first one who ever figured it out."

"I'm probably the first one fool enough to sleep with you. That must have been quite a thrill, carrying a lie that far. What would the police have done when I called them?"

"They would have said all the right things, promised to investigate and keep you informed, and then they would have covered it up. As they have for the past twenty years. But it doesn't matter, because you wouldn't have called them."

"Why? Would you have killed me first?"

He shook his head. "No. I never killed

anyone but my younger self. You wouldn't have called them because you wouldn't have wanted to hurt me. You're in love with me."

"I've said it before and I'll say it again — you're sick."

"And you're no different."

She stood there, too close to him, glaring at him. He was everything she'd ever fantasized about, he was a wretched, lying snake.

"I want to go home."

"Back to the inn?"

She shook her head. "Oh, no. You've got what you wanted. I'm leaving Hidden Harbor as soon as I can get my car."

She waited for some reaction from him, but he merely nodded. "I'll drive you back to where you left it."

"I'm not going anywhere with you. Someone else can take me."

He sighed. "Like who? We don't have taxis in Hidden Harbor. The only way you're getting back to your car is with me."

"I'm not getting anywhere near you."

"You're already quite close," he said in a soft, seductive voice, and she stumbled back nervously.

"I'll walk."

"Your ankle won't be ready for a hike

97

like that for days. Not that I wouldn't rather you stayed. Why don't you take off your clothes and get comfortable?"

She slapped him. She'd never hit anyone in her entire adult life, and the sound of her hand on his face was shocking.

He didn't even flinch. "Okay," he said. "I guess not. I'll go into town and ask someone to pick up your car and you. How about that?"

Her hand hurt, and she could see the mark on his face. It shook her, almost as much as the truth had.

"That's fine."

"Feel free to make yourself at home while I'm gone," he said. "And if you have any questions, just write them down and I'll answer them later."

"Just one. Why did you do it?"

"Why did I pretend to kill myself and take on a new persona? A dozen reasons. Maybe I didn't like myself very much. Maybe I was tired of expectations and pressure. And maybe I was tired of academics picking my bones. Like you. I like being Jacob Marley. And I sure as hell like Sydney Carton a lot better than O'Flannery."

"I hate Charles Dickens."

He sighed. "Then I guess we have a

problem." And he walked out of the house, leaving her alone.

She waited until she heard the truck drive away. The storm was over, but the ocean still tossed in angry black waves, and the sky was thick with clouds. She stood in the window, holding her breath. She didn't know if she wanted to break something or cry.

She wanted to run away and hide. Hide from Jake, hide from herself, hide from the truth. She'd made a complete and total fool of herself, and she'd ruined her career. She wasn't going to write a damned word about Michael O'Flannery. Years and years of her life had gone for nothing, done nothing but make her fall in love with a phantom.

She couldn't find her shoes, and she was going to need them if she was going to drive back to the inn. Shoes were the least of her worries. Foremost would be figuring out what she was going to say to the university. Where would her tenure track go? And did she even give a rat's ass?

She could always tell the truth. It would be the literary, academic coup of the new century.

But she wasn't going to do that. She was going to keep his secret, and she didn't even want to think why.

The need to cry seemed to be winning the battle over self-control, and she wiped her hand across her face angrily, when she heard the unmistakable sound of her Honda. It had a high-pitched sort of whistle, the fault of tricky valves, but she knew it anywhere. Jake must have found someone to pick her up.

The hell with her shoes. She headed out into the storm-wet afternoon in her bare feet, hobbling as best she could. She wanted to be gone by the time Jake got back. Though if he had any sense he'd make himself scarce until he knew she was gone. In love with him? In his dreams!

Her car was sitting in the turnaround, motor running, but there was no one in sight. She limped across the clearing, reaching for the door, when something slammed down on the back of her head and she pitched forward into utter blackness.

CHAPTER SEVEN

She was cold, she was wet, she was cramped and uncomfortable, and she had no earthly idea where she was. Scratch that, she knew where she was. On the floor in the tiny back seat of her car, in the dark, with her hands and ankles tied.

The car wasn't moving — a small consolation, until she realized that she wasn't alone. Someone was sitting in the front seat, breathing heavily. He'd adjusted the driver's seat so that it pushed against her trapped body.

Maybe Jake had changed his mind. Maybe he decided his secret was worth protecting, to the point of committing murder, and he'd picked up her car, come back to knock her out and dump her body where no one would ever find it.

It all made sense. Except that she didn't believe it. He might be a liar and a pig, but he wasn't a killer. And he wouldn't hurt her.

She shifted, and the car rocked beneath

her. "Stay still," a voice said, and Molly had a sick feeling in the pit of her stomach. It wasn't Jake, it was Davy. Of course. Davy, who was so determined to protect his friend Michael. And his friend Jake. Did he even understand what Michael had done? Did he know what he was trying to cover up?

"Davy," she said softly. "I'm uncomfortable back here. Could you untie me and let me sit up?"

"No!" He sounded fretful and frightened. "I have to do this. I don't want to, but I have to."

"What do you have to do, Davy?"

"I have to get rid of you. Jake doesn't want strangers to know. He trusts me, and I promised I'd never tell anyone about him being Michael. But you figured it out, and I can't let that happen. I have to protect him."

"I'm going away, Davy. I was just going to get my car and I was going to leave Hidden Harbor and never come back."

"But you'd tell."

"No, I wouldn't. I can keep a secret, Davy, just as you can. I'll go back to Michigan and you'll never hear from me again."

"I can't let you do that." His voice was soft, implacable. "It won't hurt, not for

102

long. Jake wouldn't like it if I hurt you. They say drowning's easy. You just sort of go to sleep."

The fear was like a cold stone in the pit of her stomach. "I don't want to drown."

"I know," Davy said in a mournful voice. "But there's no choice." He opened the car door, and the dome light came on, momentarily blinding her. It had gotten dark so quickly — how long had she been lying cramped in the back of her car? She could hear the roar and crash of the surf, and her panic grew.

He opened the back door and caught her by the shoulders, pulling her out onto the cold, wet ground. He was very strong, a huge, powerful man with the mind of a child, and there was no way she could reason with him. No way she could even begin to fight him.

He started dragging her through the mud, closer to the sound of the roaring ocean. She tried to dig in her heels, but he didn't seem to notice. He was panting slightly from the effort, but it was more of an inconvenience than anything else. Then he stopped, and put her into a sitting position. She was on the cliffs above Claussen's Cove, where Jake's parents had died.

"I'm going to have to untie you," Davy

was saying. "And I want you to promise not to run. If they find your body with your hands and feet tied they might think it wasn't an accident."

"They might," Molly agreed gravely.

"I'll be very cross with you if you run."

She said nothing as he bent over her, unfastening the binding that he had wrapped around her ankles. He'd used an old phone cord, and the plastic had dug into her sprained ankle, making it worse. He removed it, then proceeded to recoil it in a neat little circle. Molly just watched him.

He reached for her wrists and began the same process, biting his lip as he concentrated, squatting over her in the darkness. She waited until the knot loosened, and then she kicked her foot out, hard, aiming for his groin.

His shriek told her that she'd made contact. He fell backward, howling in pain, but she was already up and running, in a crazy, crablike run with her wounded ankle slowing her down, not daring to look behind her to see whether he was following her or not. She scrambled across the rocky headland, sobbing with fear, when a bank of bright lights came over the crest of the hill, blinding her.

She slid then, going down hard, when

she felt Davy's hand grab her neck. "You shouldn't have done that!" he screamed in her face. "You hurt me!"

In the distance she could hear the slamming of car doors. Lots of them. The sound of voices coming closer, the lights spearing the murky sky, illuminating the two of them as they stood perched on the edge of the cliff.

"Let her go, Davy." Jake's voice came out of the darkness, calm and soothing. "You don't want to hurt her."

"Yes, I do. She kicked me. And she's going to tell everybody about you. She knows, Jake. You can't trust her."

"Let her go," Jake said again, and even through her own terror Molly wondered whether she imagined the edge of fear in his voice. "No one's going to be mad at you, I promise. The police have promised to stay back if you'll just talk to me."

"They'll send me back to the hospital," Davy said in an aggrieved voice.

Lie to him, Molly thought desperately.

But it seemed as if Jake could only lie to her. "Just for a little while, Davy. Remember, you liked it there. You had fun. And I'll visit. All of us will."

"Okay," Davy said with one of his lightning-fast shifts of mood. His hand loosened on her neck for a moment, and Molly tensed her muscles, ready to spring away. His grip was still too tight, and she couldn't breathe, couldn't even say anything. "But first I have to kill her."

"No! Davy, you promised!" Jake said.

"Promised what?"

"You promised you would never hurt anything I cared about. Remember? You said you'd take care of the things I love."

For a moment the only sound was the roar of the surf and the faint crackling of a police radio, and the strange roaring in her ears as she struggled to breathe. And then Davy spoke. "You love her? Why, Jake?" He seemed astounded by the notion.

"I have no idea," Jake said, sounding so disgusted with himself that for one crazy moment she was tempted to believe him. "But I do. Now let her go, Davy, and come with me."

Another endless moment. Davy's fierce hold on her neck eased, and she fell on the ground in a limp heap, gasping for breath. And Davy wandered off into the night, heading for Jake.

CHAPTER EIGHT

She didn't see Jake again. With the entire police force of Hidden Harbor fussing over her, she didn't have the wit or the nerve to ask where he'd gone. Not until they brought her to the emergency room to be checked over, not until she was released into Laura Jane Twitchell's care, did she finally ask.

"Oh, Jake went with Davy to the state hospital," Laura Jane said cheerfully. "He promised Davy he wouldn't leave him until he got settled, and Jake always keeps his promises."

"Jake," Molly echoed in a cynical voice.

"That's what we call him. That's who he is now, and happier for it. I'd hate to see anything happen to his peace of mind."

She limped over to Laura Jane's van. "So what are you going to do, try to throw me over a cliff if I don't agree?"

Laura Jane laughed. "We all know perfectly well you wouldn't harm Jake. Davy's not quite right, you know. He doesn't see things so clearly."

"You're wrong. There's nothing I'd like better than to cause some major damage to the man," Molly said bitterly.

Laura Jane grinned. "Lover's quarrel?" she asked. "I remember what that's like. You don't like it that he lied to you, and I don't blame you. I knew the moment you walked into the diner that you two were made for each other. You need to —"

"I need to leave," Molly interrupted her.

Laura Jane looked stricken. "You can't! Your car's still in police custody. It's evidence —"

"I can rent a car. I don't know if I ever want to get in that one again. How do I rent a car?"

"I think you should wait until Jake gets back. Marjorie told me to bring you back. She's made a nice dinner for you, and you need a good night's sleep. In the morning, if you're still set on leaving we can call Doris Perkins down at the garage. They sometimes rent cars."

"I'm not waiting. I'm only going back to the inn to pack."

"It's almost nine o'clock at night! You can't leave. Not after all you've been through. It's been a hell of a day."

You don't know the half of it, Molly thought, feeling a faint blush stain her face. And that was exactly why she had to get away from here. "I can drive as far as Portland and spend the night," she said. "I'm not spending another night in Hidden Harbor. I hate it here."

"No, you don't," Laura Jane said wisely. "But I understand why you're upset. Maybe you just need some time to yourself to understand what you really do want."

"I know what I want. I want Michael O'Flannery to be dead so I can write about him and get tenure. Since that's not about to happen, I'm going to go back to work early and see if I can figure out what I'm going to do."

Laura Jane just looked at her. "You're as stubborn as my kids. There's no way I can talk you out of this, is there?"

"No way."

She sighed. "In that case, I'll call Doris tonight. She'll find a car you can take."

"I won't be bringing it back."

"Don't worry about it. She'll make arrangements."

She passed him on the road coming into town, three hours later. It was after midnight, and she was crying so hard she could barely see, but in the brightness of her headlights the truck was instantly recognizable. She didn't know whether he saw her or not as he was driving very fast, an abstracted expression on his face.

It didn't matter, she thought, wiping her face with the back of her hand. She'd be gone, and once he was sure she wasn't going to blow his cover, he'd be happy. Not that she cared whether he was happy or not, she reminded herself, swallowing a shaky gulp. And she headed west, into the flatlands, with the ocean at her back.

It was three weeks later, Thanksgiving, the start of the Christmas season, and Molly was not in a festive spirit. She'd made some weak excuse to her family in Rhode Island — she couldn't face the holidays at the moment, couldn't face her overachieving siblings and her academic parents. Not when she was ready to make the hardest decision of her life.

She was going to the ocean. The Pacific Ocean, as far away from Maine as she could get. She was leaving her job and her tenure track, and she didn't give a damn where she ended up. She had enough money to tide her over for the time being, and maybe she'd find a job teaching, maybe she wouldn't. The main thing was to get over Jake.

Time was supposed to cure everything.

It was doing a piss-poor job of curing her depression. If she still had a romantic bone in her body she'd call it a broken heart, but she decided that was giving it more importance than it deserved. It was no wonder she was having a hard time. She'd nearly been killed. She'd been tricked and lied to. And her career had imploded in front of her very eyes, and she'd had no choice but to let it.

The fact that she dreamed about Jake was merely an unfortunate side effect. A little Prozac, a little sunshine and she'd be fine, just fine.

Her apartment was already packed. She'd put most of her furniture in storage, keeping only her bed and her television for the last few days. She made herself a cup of coffee and turned on the TV. The Macy's parade was winding down, Santa Claus was about to arrive, and Molly felt the damned tears start again. She cried over the most ridiculous things. Beer commercials. Songs on the radio. Pictures of kittens. It wasn't surprising that Santa Claus would do it to her.

She switched the channel, ending up on the Weather Channel. She watched it dully. It was cold and rainy along the coast of Maine. As if she gave a damn. She wanted them to have blizzards and tornadoes and volcanoes. She wanted them to disappear in a puff of smoke.

No, not them. Him. Just Jacob Marley and the chains he forged in life.

The day went from bad to worse. She turned on *It's a Wonderful Life* and fell asleep in front of the television. When she awoke, the room was dark and *A Christmas Carol* was on. All she needed was to see the ghost of Jacob Marley rattling his chains when she would have happily wrapped them around his neck. She sat up, dazed and groggy from too much sleep, when she heard the knocking at her door.

She groaned. With her luck one of her well-meaning neighbors would be stopping by with leftover turkey, and she wasn't in the mood. She was indulging herself in misery and having a fine time doing it. Later she'd put on something mournful and have a stormy cry, but in the meantime she wanted to watch TV and say nasty things to Jacob Marley's ghost without having to explain herself to anyone.

The knock came again, and she considered staying put, then realized she had the TV turned up loud enough that she wouldn't get away with it. And whoever was out there was getting more and more irritated. She could tell by the sound of his fist on the door.

"Coming. Hold your horses!" she said irritably, struggling to her feet. She was wearing sweats, a baggy T-shirt, and her hair was in braids, and she couldn't care less who saw her that way. Until she opened the door and looked up into his dark blue eyes.

The silence was palpable, with only the muffled sound of Scrooge in the background. "You look like hell," Jake said charitably.

She slammed the door in his face.

She knew it wasn't going to end at that, but it was extremely satisfying. She waited a good two minutes, then finally opened the door again.

He looked the same. Grumpy, sexy, annoying as hell. Now that she knew just what that mouth tasted like, it was even more unsettling, but she plastered a steely expression on her face and opened the door wider. "You're bothering the neighbors."

He stepped inside, closing it behind him. She hadn't told him he could, but that seemed beside the point. "Why are you here?" she demanded.

"Mabel Barton is pregnant."

Molly blinked. "How nice. Are you the father?"

She'd forgotten his laugh. "Not likely. Mabel and Frank already have five little monsters, and I don't think Frank would take it too well if I messed around with his wife."

"And how does this concern me? Not that I'd care if you were messing around with her," she added hastily.

She thought she'd memorized everything about him. And she had, but the reality of that little half smile hit her with the power of a sledgehammer.

"Of course you wouldn't," he said soothingly. "Mabel teaches high school English in Hidden Harbor. She's taking her maternity leave after Christmas."

"And . . . ?"

"And we need someone to fill in for her. I thought you might be needing a job."

"And you drove twelve hundred miles to ask me this?" she said in disbelief.

"Actually I flew. I thought we could drive back together."

He looked so innocent. As if he were simply doing his civic duty. "And I would want to because . . . ?" she prompted him.

"Because you like teaching and you're out of a job."

She didn't bother asking him how he knew that. "I can find another one closer."

"Because you want to live by the ocean again."

"I was planning on moving to California."

"California's for wimps. You're tough enough to handle Maine."

"Am I?"

"You're tough enough to handle me."

She didn't argue with that. "If I wanted to," she said.

"If you wanted to," he agreed. "So what do you think?"

"What do you think?" she countered.

He took a deep breath. "I think that I can't spend another day waiting for you to come back, and if worse comes to worse I'll follow you to California, but I really think things would work out better if you just gave up and came back with me."

"Gave up?"

"Gave up being pissed at me. Gave up being proud."

"And what are you giving up?"

"My freedom. Come back with me, Molly."

"Why?"

"You're going to make me say it, aren't you?"

"Yes."

He looked furious, frustrated and undeniably gorgeous. "All right, I admit it. For want of a better word, I'm in love with you."

"I don't know if there is a better word," she said, suddenly feeling very calm.

"So will you? Come back with me? Or am I going to have to stay here in this god-awful flat landscape?"

She smiled up at him. He hadn't touched her, deliberately, because he knew when he did she couldn't think straight. She reached up and cupped his face with her hands. "On one condition," she said.

His eyes burned down into hers. "Anything," he said.

"You change your name again. I really do hate Charles Dickens."

And she let out a shriek of laughter as he scooped her up in his arms.

ABOUT THE AUTHOR

Anne Stuart has written over sixty novels in her more than twenty-five years as a writer. She has won every major award in the business, including three RITA® Awards from Romance Writers of America, as well as their Lifetime Achievement Award. Anne's books continue to make national and chain bestseller lists, and she has been quoted in *People, USA Today* and *Vogue.* When she's not writing or traveling around the country speaking to various writers' groups, she can be found at home in northern Vermont with her husband and two children.

We hope you have enjoyed this Large Print book. Other Thorndike, Wheeler or Chivers Press Large Print books are available at your library or directly from the publishers.

For more information about current and up-coming titles, please call or write, without obligation, to:

Publisher
Thorndike Press
295 Kennedy Memorial Drive
Waterville, ME   04901
Tel. (800) 223-1244

Or visit our Web site at:
www.gale.com/thorndike
www.gale.com/wheeler

OR

Chivers Large Print
published by BBC Audiobooks Ltd
St James House, The Square
Lower Bristol Road
Bath BA2 3SB
England
Tel. +44(0) 800 136919
email: bbcaudiobooks@bbc.co.uk
www.bbcaudiobooks.co.uk

All our Large Print titles are designed for easy reading, and all our books are made to last.